Robert Smalls Sails to FREEDOM

by Susan Taylor Brown

illustrations by Felicia Marshall

Millbrook Press/Minneapolis

The author would like to thank Ms. Kitt Haley Alexander, founder and chair of Robert Smalls Legacy Foundation, Inc., and Marjorie McNinch, reference archivist at the Hagley Museum and Library, for their invaluable help with this book. Special thanks to Kitt for reading the manuscript and to my editor, Laura Waxman, for helping me bring the story to life.

Millbrook Press
A division of Lerner Publishing Group
241 First Avenue North
Minneapolis, MN 55401 U.S.A.

Website address: www.lernerbooks.com

Library of Congress Cataloging-in-Publication Data

Brown, Susan Taylor, 1958–
    Robert Smalls sails to freedom / by Susan Taylor Brown ; illustrations by Felicia Marshall.
      p.   cm. — (On my own history)
    ISBN-13: 978–1–57505–872–6 (lib. bdg. : alk. paper)
    ISBN-10: 1–57505–872–3 (lib. bdg. : alk. paper)
    1. Smalls, Robert, 1839–1915—Juvenile literature. 2. African Americans—Biography—Juvenile literature. 3. Fugitive slaves—United States—Biography—Juvenile literature. 4. United States—History—Civil War, 1861–1865—Participation, African American—Juvenile literature. I. Marshall, Felicia, ill. II. Title. III. Series.
    E185.97.S6B76 2006
    973.8'092—dc22   2005013034

Manufactured in the United States of America
1 2 3 4 5 6 – JR – 11 10 09 08 07 06

For soldiers everywhere.
And for Erik, always
—S.T.B.

I dedicate this book to my children Elijah, Maya, and Caleb.
—F.M.

Beaufort,
South Carolina, 1847

Robert followed Mr. McKee
out to the river.
Robert carried
a fishing pole.
Mr. McKee walked fast.
Robert hurried to keep up.

At the river,

Robert hooked a worm on the pole.

Then he handed the pole to Mr. McKee.

Mr. McKee was going to have

a fine day of fishing.

But it was not a fine day for Robert.

It was just another day of work.

Like most black people in the South,

Robert Smalls was a slave.

He belonged to his master, Mr. McKee.

Robert worked in the master's house.

He carried firewood

and ran errands.

He helped Mr. McKee

into and out of his carriage.

He even carried his master's gun

on hunting trips.

Robert was a good slave,

and Mr. McKee treated him well.

But Robert knew that slaves

could be bought and sold at any time.

Mr. McKee could sell him too.

Mr. McKee also owned Robert's mother.

Lydia Smalls wanted a better life for her son.

She wanted him always to remember

the hardships of slavery.

That way, he might someday

fight for his freedom.

Robert's mother made her son watch slaves

being sold in town.

Sometimes angry owners whipped the slaves.
Many slaves wore heavy iron circles chained
to their ankles.
The iron kept them from running away.
Lydia told Robert that some black people
tried to escape to the free North.
Slavery was against the law there.
Robert learned to hate slavery.
He began to dream of freedom.

Charleston, South Carolina, 1851

Robert had turned twelve years old.
Mr. McKee wanted him to get a job.
Robert's master planned to keep
all the money Robert earned.
Mr. McKee sent Robert alone
to the city of Charleston.
Robert had to leave his mother behind.

He got a job as a waiter in a fancy hotel.

He earned five dollars each month.

Every penny went to Mr. McKee.

Next, he got a job as a lamplighter.

He didn't keep that money, either.

Mr. McKee took it all.

Robert was a long way from being free.

In his spare time,
Robert went to the waterfront.
He loved to watch the ships sail
in and out of Charleston Harbor.

He talked to the workers who unloaded
cargo from boats and ships.
They told Robert about faraway places
where black people were free.
More than ever,
Robert longed for his freedom.

Soon Robert got permission
from Mr. McKee to change jobs.
He wanted to learn the sailing trade.
Day after day,
Robert worked on the waterfront.
He learned how to make sails
and paint ships.
He learned how to read maps of the river
and not get lost.

He learned how to sail a ship
through narrow waterways
and not run into rocks.
Robert became an excellent sailor.
He could steer a ship
as well as any white pilot.
But his master still got all the money
that Robert earned.
And Robert still dreamed of being free.

When Robert was 17,

he married a slave named Hannah.

He still worked for Mr. McKee.

But Robert was allowed to keep

a little money for himself.

Still, Robert was not happy.

He and his wife still belonged

to white owners.

Even his new baby, Elizabeth Lydia,

belonged to Hannah's master.

They could each be sold

to different owners at any time.

Then they might lose each other forever.

Robert hated that.

He wanted to keep his family safe.

One day, Robert went to see
Hannah's master.
Mr. Kingman agreed to sell Hannah
and Elizabeth's freedom for $800.
That was a lot of money.
It would take Robert and Hannah
years to save it.

But Robert was determined.

Then he and Hannah had another baby.

They named him Robert Jr.

They would need even more money

to buy this baby's freedom.

Would they ever be free?

Robert had new hope in 1861.

That year, a war broke out between

the free North and the slaveholding South.

The North was called the Union.

The South called itself the Confederacy.

If the Union won this Civil War,

slavery might end forever.

The Union fought battles with

the Confederates all over the South.

They even fought

near Charleston Harbor.

Robert heard stories about slaves who
escaped to nearby Union armies or ships.
The Union protected many slaves
and gave them freedom.
Robert wanted to escape with his family. It
would not be easy.
But he knew he had to find a way.

July 1861,
Charleston

During the war, Robert got a new job.
He worked with other slaves on
a powerful steamboat called the *Planter*.
The Confederates were using it to deliver
messages and supplies to forts onshore.
The forts held soldiers
preparing for battle.

Guards at the forts watched
for enemy ships.
Before any ship could pass a fort,
it had to whistle the secret signal.
That way, guards could tell who was
an enemy and who was a friend.

Every day, Robert watched the ship's
captain give the signal at each fort.
Captain Relyea gave two long pulls
and one short pull of the ship's whistle.
Sometimes the captain
waved at the guards.
Then he stood with his arms crossed
and waited to pass.
Robert remembered everything he saw.

One day, the slave crew was alone
on the *Planter*.
Someone made a joke
about stealing the ship.
Everyone laughed.
Robert laughed too.
Then he got an idea.

Union ships were just outside the harbor.
Robert saw them every day he went out
on the *Planter.*
He and the black crew could try to escape
to a Union ship on the *Planter.*
Robert could steer the ship
as well as Captain Relyea.
Did they dare take the chance?

Robert told Hannah about his idea.

They both knew they might be killed

if they were caught.

But they both longed to be free.

And they both dreamed of raising

their children in freedom.

Hannah agreed to go

wherever Robert went.

Some of the other black crew members
also agreed to escape with Robert.
They met at his home to make plans.
They chose Robert to lead the escape.
They promised to be ready
at a moment's notice.
Then they waited.

Charleston Harbor,
May 13, 1862

Robert whispered to the other slaves
to light the *Planter*'s fires.
They needed to make steam
to power the ship.
It was time to escape!

The ship's white officers had decided
to spend the night on land.
They left cannons on the *Planter*
to be delivered to Confederate forts.
But Robert had other plans.
He was taking the cannons with him.
He wanted to give them and
the powerful *Planter* to the Union.

31

In the darkness of early morning,

Robert sailed the *Planter* out of the dock.

He stopped at a nearby dock to pick up

Hannah, Elizabeth Lydia, and Robert Jr.

Four more women and another child
also came aboard.
Hannah held Robert Jr. close
to keep him from crying.

Robert knew the ship could be captured
at any moment.
Soldiers with guns stood guard
at all the forts.
Their cannons were always ready to fire.
But Robert had a plan.
He was going to disguise himself
as Captain Relyea.

Robert wore a good jacket.

He put on the captain's hat.

Then he stood behind

the captain's wheel.

He hoped his disguise would work.

Soon the *Planter* came to the first fort.
Everyone on the ship was depending
on Robert.
If the Confederates caught them,
they might all be killed.
Robert took a deep breath.
He thought about the lessons his mother
had taught him.
He thought about his family.
He thought about freedom.

Then Robert gave the signal,
two long pulls and a jerk of the whistle.
He waited.
Would the soldiers fire at them?
The guns remained silent.
The *Planter* passed on by.
Robert and the other slaves sailed
closer to freedom.

Each time Robert passed another fort,
he gave two long pulls
and a jerk of the whistle.
And each time, Confederate guards
let the *Planter* pass on by.

Soon the sun began to rise.

Robert had a new problem.

His disguise might not work
in daylight.

He had to find a way
to hide the color of his skin.

The ship reached the last fort
at daybreak.
Robert moved back into the shadows.
He tipped his hat down over his eyes
and waved at the guard.
He gave the signal one last time.
Then Robert crossed his arms and waited,
just like he had seen the captain do.
The guard signaled back.
The *Planter* was allowed to pass!
They were almost safe.

The U.S.S. *Onward* was the first
Union ship Robert saw.
It guarded all the other Union ships
from the enemy.
Robert ordered his crew to raise
a white flag on the Confederate *Planter*.
The flag was a signal to the *Onward*
that the *Planter* came in peace.
Then the *Planter* headed straight
for the *Onward*.
Suddenly, Confederate soldiers onshore
saw the ship head out to sea.

42

They tried to shoot down the runaway ship.

But they were too late.

The *Planter* was already too far away.

Robert and the others weren't safe yet.

The sailors on the *Onward* had not seen

the *Planter*'s white flag.

They thought the Confederate ship was

attacking their ship.

They pointed their cannons

straight at Robert and his family.

Robert quickly turned the ship's wheel.

The white flag billowed in the wind.

The Union captain ordered his men
to stop their attack.
Then Robert guided the *Planter*
close enough to shout a greeting.
"Good morning, sir.
I've brought you some of the old
United States' guns, sir!"

Robert looked out past the Union ships.

Slavery was behind him.

Freedom awaited.

His family was safe.

And his heart felt free.

Afterword

By turning the *Planter* over to Admiral Samuel F. Du Pont, Robert became a hero. The U.S. government awarded prize money to him and the rest of the black crew. And Robert went right to work for the Union cause. For the rest of the war, Robert bravely piloted ships for the Union's navy and army. On December 1, 1863, he was promoted to captain of the *Planter*.

Although Robert lived as a free man, he and all slaves in the United States were not officially freed until the North won the Civil War in 1865. After the war, Robert bought the old McKee house, where he had once lived as a slave.

In South Carolina, Robert learned to read and write. He helped draft South Carolina's constitution, became a state senator, and then was elected to the U.S. House of Representatives for five terms. As a lawmaker, he fought for the rights of African Americans. In 1889, he was appointed U.S. Collector of Customs in Beaufort, South Carolina. He held this job for 20 years.

Robert died on February 23, 1915, at the age of 75. A bust near his grave reads:

My race needs no special defense,
for the past history of them in this country
proves them to be the equal of any people anywhere.
All they need is an equal chance in the battle of life.

Select Bibliography

Brown, William Wells. *The Negro in the American Rebellion: His Heroism and His Fidelity*. New York: Citadel Press, 1971.

Charleston Daily Courier, "The Steamer Planter." May 15, 1862.

Du Pont, Samuel F., to his wife, Sophie Madeleine Du Pont. May 13, 1862.

Garrison, Webb. *Creative Minds in Desperate Times*. Nashville: Rutledge Press, 1997.

Guthrie, James M. *Camp-Fires of the Afro-American*. New York: Johnson Reprint Corporation, 1970. First published 1899 by Afro-American Publishing Co.

Harpers Weekly, "The Steamer 'Planter' and her Captor." June 14, 1862.

Miller, Edward A., Jr. *Gullah Statesman: Robert Smalls from Slavery to Congress, 1839–1915*. Columbia: University of South Carolina Press, 1995.

New York Daily Tribune, "Robert Smalls." May 20, 1862.

New York Daily Tribune, "Robert Smalls, the Negro Pilot." September 10, 1862.

New York Times, "The Hero of the Planter." October 3, 1862.

New York Times, "News of the Day: The Rebellion." May 18, 1862.

Quarles, Benjamin. *The Negro in the Civil War*. New York: Da Capo Press, 1989.

Robert Smalls Legacy Foundation. *Official Robert Smalls' Website and Information Center*. http://www.robertsmalls.org.

Simmons, William J. *Men of Mark*. New York: Arno Press, 1968. First published 1887 by O. G. M. Redwell & Co.

Uya, Okon Edet. *From Slavery to Public Service: Robert Smalls, 1839–1915*. New York: Oxford University Press, 1971.

A note about the quotations: Robert's words on page 45 come from *Camp-Fires of the Afro-American*; the quotation on page 47 was spoken by Robert at the South Carolina Constitutional Convention in 1895, as quoted in *Gullah Statesman*.